SNOW WHITE AND ROSE RED

by the
Brothers Grimm

Illustrated by
James Weren

Troll Associates

Troll Associates, Mahwah, N.J.

Library of Congress Catalog Card Number: 78-18074
ISBN 0-89375-136-7

Once there was a poor widow who lived in a little house at the edge of the woods. In the front yard she had two rosebushes—one with white flowers, and one with red flowers. The woman's two daughters were named Snow White and Rose Red, because they were as beautiful as the flowers.

Snow White and Rose Red were very good children. The two girls loved each other very much, and they shared everything they had.

Rose Red straightened the house every morning in the summer, and picked flowers for her mother. Snow White lighted the fire every morning in the winter, and put the kettle on. And on snowy winter evenings, the two girls sat by the hearth, spinning and listening to their mother read.

One evening, they heard a knock at the door. It was a huge brown bear! Snow White and Rose Red tried to hide, but the bear said, "Please do not be afraid. All I want is to come in out of the cold."

"You poor thing!" cried the mother. "Come in and warm yourself by the fire. But don't get too close, or you will burn your furry coat." Then she said to her daughters, "This bear is our friend, and will not hurt us. Come and welcome our guest."

So the girls brushed the snow from the bear's coat, and he lay down in front of the fire. Soon Snow White and Rose Red were playing merrily with their new friend. They pulled at his coat and rolled him over with their feet. And when they were too rough, he laughed, "Please do not hurt me."

That night, the bear slept by the fire. In the morning, the girls let him out, and he plodded off into the snowy forest. But every evening after that, he returned and curled up before the fire.

When the snow finally melted, the bear said, "Now it is time for me to leave you."

Snow White was sorry to hear this. "But where will you go?" she asked.

The bear replied, "I must go into the woods to protect my treasures from the evil dwarfs. In the winter, they stay in their underground homes because the ground is frozen. But now the ground is soft. They will dig their way up, and steal whatever they find."

Snow White was so sad that she opened the door very slowly. As the bear hurried out, he bumped against the latch, and ripped a small hole in his coat. Snow White thought she saw something shining through the hole, but she was not sure.

Later, Snow White and Rose Red went into the forest to gather wood for the fire. They came upon an ugly old dwarf, who was dancing and hopping up and down next to a big log.

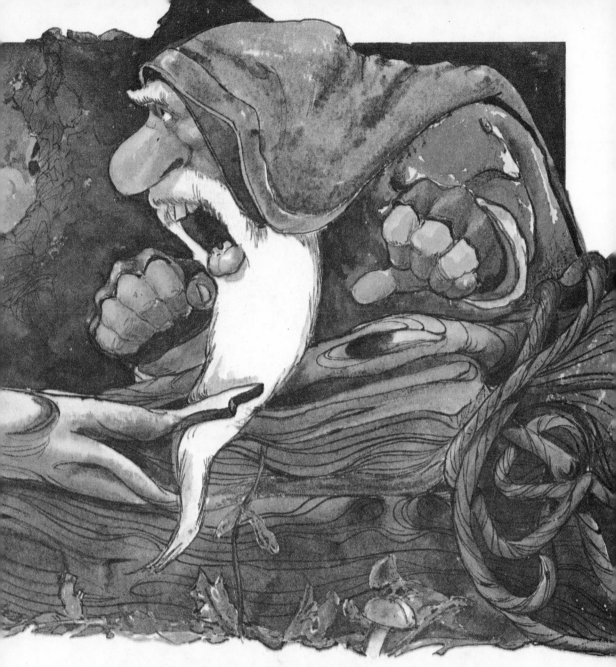

"Well, don't just stand there!" cried the dwarf. "Any stupid goose can see that my beard is caught! Help me get it free!" Then the two sisters took hold of the dwarf's beard, and pulled and tugged. But it was no use.

"You blockheads!" cried the dwarf. "Do something!" So Snow White took out her scissors and cut off the very tip of the dwarf's beard. This made the ugly little man very angry. "A curse on you!" he screamed. Then he picked up a bag of gold and went away, muttering, "How rude you are to snip the tip of my beautiful beard."

Some time later, Snow White and Rose Red saw the same ugly dwarf dancing and jumping at the edge of a stream.

"Oh, be careful!" cried the girls. "You might fall in!"

"I am not *that* slow-witted!" screamed the dwarf. "Any simpleton can see that my beard is caught in this fishing line! And now a big fish is trying to pull me into the water. If you weren't so stupid, you would try to help me!"

The two sisters tried to untangle the dwarf's beard from the fishing line. But it was no use. So Snow White took out her scissors, and cut off another piece of his beard.

"You toadstool!" he screamed. "Look what you did! You cut off the best part!" Then he snatched a bag of pearls, and disappeared behind a rock.

Several days later, Snow White and Rose Red went into town to fetch some needles and pins and ribbons and lace for their mother. On the way, they passed a pile of rocks. A huge bird swooped down behind the rocks, and a loud screech filled the air.

The bird had seized the ugly little dwarf, and was trying to carry him away. The two sisters grabbed the dwarf, and held him as tightly as they could. At last, the bird let go and flew away.

"You clumsy donkeys!" cried the dwarf. "You made me rip my jacket! Can't you do *anything* right? What a dreadful bother you are!" Then he swung a bag of jewels onto his shoulder, and hurried into a cave in the rocks.

On the way back from town, Snow White and Rose Red came to a clearing. The ugly old dwarf had spread out his treasures on the ground, where they sparkled in the sun. The girls stopped to admire the jewels.

"What! You again?" cried the dwarf, in a terrible rage. "What are you staring at? Get along and mind your own business."

Suddenly, a huge bear came into the clearing. The dwarf jumped to his feet, and tried to get away. But the bear was too fast for him.

"Let me go!" begged the dwarf. "If you do, I will give you all these treasures! I am too old and tough to make a good meal for you. Take those two wicked girls instead! They are plump and tender, and should taste delicious!"

The bear did not say a word, but swung his huge paw in a powerful blow. The ugly old dwarf fell to the ground and did not move.

Snow White and Rose Red hurried away. But the bear called out, "Snow White! Rose Red! Wait for me!" The girls stopped at once, for they knew that voice. It belonged to the bear who had spent so many nights by their fire.

As the bear came toward the two sisters, his furry coat fell to the ground, and a handsome young prince stood before them! He was dressed in golden clothes that shined brightly in the sun.

"I am the son of a rich king," said the prince. "An evil dwarf stole my treasures and cast a spell on me. I was doomed to roam the forest as a bear, but now the spell is broken."

And so Snow White married the prince, and Rose
Red married his brother. They lived in a huge castle, and
their mother came to stay with them. She planted her two
rosebushes in front of the castle, and they bloomed every
year with the loveliest red and white roses.